Joanna Hill was born in Oxford. She has subsequently lived in London, New York, Monaco and France. She likes to set her novels in one of these places all of which she knows very well. Her interests are fairly broad: racing, some sports and Egyptian archaeology. The last being as the result of excavating in Egypt whilst working in New York.

Gemma Jones who, as before, has sorted me out technically and the staff at Austin Macauley Publishing for being so helpful.

Joanna Hill

NOT ANOTHER MURDER, PLEASE!

Austin Macauley Publishers

LONDON · CAMBRIDGE · NEW YORK · SHARJAH

Copyright © Joanna Hill 2025

The right of Joanna Hill to be identified as author of this work has been asserted by the author in accordance with sections 77 and 78 of the Copyright, Designs and Patents Act 1988.

All rights reserved. No part of this publication may be reproduced, stored in a retrieval system, or transmitted in any form or by any means, electronic, mechanical, photocopying, recording, or otherwise, without the prior permission of the publishers.

Any person who commits any unauthorised act in relation to this publication may be liable to criminal prosecution and civil claims for damages.

This is a work of fiction. Names, characters, businesses, places, events, locales, and incidents are either the products of the author's imagination or used in a fictitious manner. Any resemblance to actual persons, living or dead, or actual events is purely coincidental.

A CIP catalogue record for this title is available from the British Library.

ISBN 9781035885541 (Paperback)
ISBN 9781035885558 (ePub e-book)

www.austinmacauley.com

First Published 2025
Austin Macauley Publishers Ltd®
1 Canada Square
Canary Wharf
London
E14 5AA

Prologue

Laurel Park is a large mid Georgian mansion with an earlier, Elizabethan wing. It had been rescued from possible post World War Two destruction, by its purchase and conversion into a retirement home.

Chapter One

In the huge fireplace, although it was quite warm outside, the fire crackled and popped waking up the man who was dozing at his desk. 'Shit' he mumbled aloud as he picked up his pen again. He was editing a proof for the next house newsletter. How on earth could he lure some more people to move in while there was such a shortage of elderly men around; had they all been killed off by their fiercesome wives? He knew all about them!

Peter mentally ran through the present residents of Laurel Park. On the whole, you would think they were all pretty sprightly—or if that was not the precise word—in fairly good health, for their ages which ranged from mid-seventies to mid-nineties. In fact, the most elderly pair were a remarkably nimble ninety-three, Geoff and Julia! He wondered aloud, 'will I be like them when I get to their ages? Probably not! Probably be long dead and buried by then!'

His eyes scanned the draft. He knew he should be doing all this on his computer but somehow, he'd come rather late in life (He'd been at least forty) to the modern age and could only do the simplest tasks on his machine. His daughters pulled his leg unmercifully about his lack of technical know-how and, when they came home, he always had various tangles which they had to sort out for him. However, he noticed that both of them came home pretty often and it could not have been solely that he was a generous Dad; their mother was somewhere unspecified, possibly in the Far East, with a toy boy who seemed to be the same age as the girls' own boyfriends.

He tried to think of something else to add to the house newsletter. Were there any birthdays or anniversaries approaching? He kept a sort of crib sheet where he had noted most of these dates, but he needed to keep it up to date or someone, particularly touchy, would be annoyed. He 'excavated' the pile of papers on his desk before laying his hand on the one he needed.

'Yes, yes,' he muttered under his breath, it was Lavender Hodges' 85th in two days' time; he'd better alert the kitchen. Temporarily bereft of any inspiration, he got up and, after a quick look out of the window at the pouring rain, shrugged his way into his jacket and made his way downstairs to the kitchen. Several years of experience led him to keep a sharp lookout as he went, in order to avoid an ambush by either Primrose Jones or Lady Morag both of whom always had a string of complaints and or impossible requests. He smiled to himself over some of the Christian names of the residents; his own mother had been "Violet" but today it seemed very old-fashioned and flowers as names generally seemed to be way out of date.

He turned a corner to the kitchens; his arrival heralded by a loud crashing of china accompanied by several fruity French oaths. Peter sighed as he hoped that Georges, his Chef, was not in a bad temper. This occurred quite frequently and was generally provoked by a complaint from one of the residents, most of whom were deeply conservative in their tastes and regarded with distrust anything he served with a French name, this despite the fact that they would have gobbled it down should it have appeared on the menu as it's English equivalent! He sighed, muttering under his breath, 'bon jour Georges!'

He arrived in the large kitchen with a smile pinned on his face. It was impossible, however, to entirely ignore the large quantity of broken china scattered on the floor.

'Do I need my bank card,' he tried a rather feeble joke. 'Perhaps we'd better invest in some plastic stuff!'

'Sorry, Boss!' A rather unusually apologetic Georges.

'I've just come down to see if everything is OK with you, Georges, and to discuss what we can do for Mme Lavender's birthday. Also, I just wanted to remind you of the play that's being performed here this evening. I think it would be a friendly gesture if we provide some snacks for the actors. Would this be possible? There will be about ten or twelve of their group including the stage setters etc.'

Peter was not too worried about putting the snacks on to Georges because the chef loved being involved in parties where guests were often much more appreciative of his food than some of the whining residents.

Georges smiled, he understood when he was being 'buttered up' by the Boss, and his head was already whirling with ideas for creative nibbles. As if making amends for the tray of china now lying scattered in fragments on the kitchen floor, he proposed a showy if not too pricey menu for Lavender's lunch party.

'What's the play they're doing?' the Frenchman asked.

'Oh, I'm not too sure but we've sold a lot of tickets to outsiders so I'm hoping it will be something good. I think it's probably the usual murder, who dunnit sort of thing; that always goes down well here as you know.'

'*Tres Bien!*'

Peter left the kitchen and was amused to hear Chef's voice calling up his number one *washer upper*, Hazel, to come and clear up the broken china. He was always a bit surprised, but grateful, that Georges stayed at Laurel Park and asked himself if there was a reason that, so far, he had not worked out. The sole downside apart from his periodic, temperamental bursts of anger, was that, in common with French people the world over, the Chef always took August off and it was not always easy to find cover for him. Once, Peter had found himself in the kitchen and the menus had turned into sort of boy scout camp food. He giggled to himself as he remembered one of the oldest residents, Kenneth Woodcock, saying it was the best food he'd had in a long time after a supper of fish'n chips—soggy—imported from the local village. One must be flexible running a show such as this, Peter told himself. It also paid to have a sense of humour!

Some of the residents had led interesting lives and many of them were widely travelled although Peter had discovered that none of them had ever bothered to learn a foreign language; very English he thought. They were a good bunch, on the whole, although he felt he might not be responsible for his actions if he had to listen, yet again, to Reg's story of how the Maharajah of Singh had given him a horse some fifty years ago; the snag being that the horse was perpetually lame! He was also pretty fed up with hearing about Primrose Jones' parents being invited to a Garden Party at Buckingham Palace about forty years in the past! Never mind, he abjured himself sharply, these tales don't harm you so just pin on a smile and nod.

He crossed the front hall under the benign gaze of some of his ancestors and went out. The rain had stopped and all that remained to remind him of the wettest month in hundreds of years was the steady drip, drip of water from the gutters. Odd thoughts popped up, unasked, such as he must get Hodges, the groundsman, to tip some water out of the butts; they were all overflowing and pools of water were lying across the gravel sweep in front of the house.

What needed doing first now that the rain had ceased for the time being? Well, certainly the tennis court needed attention. It had been impossible to mow recently but it certainly required a cut not to mention a session with the heavy roller and then there would be marking up. He mentally assigned this chore to the new young man he had just hired for the summer. Sam lived in the village and he was due to go to Durham University in September; he had leaped at the chance to work at Laurel Place in the summer. Peter had put him in charge of the tennis court, the swimming pool and the croquet lawn as his priorities. Peter ran his eye, mentally, down the present list of residents; not too many sports people or whatever stupid new name they came under these days, although croquet was quite popular with the men. He smiled as he thought of the big row that had taken place on the croquet lawn at the end of the previous summer with a dispute between usually henpecked Ron (husband to Lady Moira) and the somewhat hot-tempered Reginald Smyth. It had almost turned into a disaster when the worm had turned and Ron had raised his mallet in a very threatening manner over Reg.

Fortunately, or not according to your point of view, thought Peter, Primrose Jones had been watching the match and threw her extremely small, slight body at Ron; he'd dropped the mallet with an apology, but Reg cursing at 'interfering old women' had stumped off muttering words to the effect that he had been about to retaliate and rid the world of, probably, its greatest bore. The two men did not speak since that day!

Peter had been a bit nervous of the two men resurrecting their quarrel, but fortunately, winter had intervened and croquet had finished for the year. Now with summer approaching, he'd better warn Sam to keep his eye open for any more signs of croquet-rage. He tapped his teeth with his finger as he scanned the gardens for Hodges, groundsman and general muscle-man.

He pulled his phone out of his pocket and looked at his diary; he'd suddenly remembered that he hadn't yet fixed a date for the annual croquet match against Green Lawns. Green Lawns is a retirement home quite nearby that considers itself rather posh, quite why Peter had no idea! Would he risk Reg playing was a burning question. Of course, it was ridiculous to cancel the match because two of his elderly, octogenarian residents had fallen out. Or was it? He remembered with relief that he had both of his daughters staying the coming weekend and he decided he would chew it over with them. His wife having taken off (or been thrown out, according to one's point of view,) several years previously, he occasionally felt the need for a sounding board and the girls were very handy for this. He did really feel that the two of them 'had his corner.'

Chapter Two

He did a quick tour of the gardens nearest to the house. Everything looked in good order and all the plants he'd bought to add to the borders for the summer were growing busily and were going to make a colourful show in a few weeks' time so long as the heavens didn't open every day; that, of course, remained to be seen. He'd been keeping a diary over the past three years as to the flowering habits of the most reliable perennials. There was no doubt that everything was way ahead of a few years ago; global warming was not a question any longer, it had become a reality. He knew there were still a number of "deniers", but in his book the evidence was clear. What would it be like if and when he had grandchildren?

His phone burbled. It was Tiffany, his elder daughter.

'Hi, Dad. You OK?' she asked. Not waiting for a reply, she added, 'I'm coming down this evening because I seem to recall that you said you were going to have a play on Saturday.'

'Yes, Darling, we are having 'Dial M for Murder' this evening, put on by the local thespians—you know the gang who come several times a year. I always think that, in fact, it gives them more pleasure producing these plays than it gives the residents who are the audience but that is a horrible and cynical thing to say I know!'

'Am Drams!' laughed Tiffany. 'I know what you mean but I expect we'll enjoy it all the same. Is Jem coming?'

'She hasn't told me but that doesn't mean much I know. I think she has a new man in her life so I expect it depends on him.'

'Right, well I'll see you for supper. Bye!' She was gone.

He walked slowly back to the house thinking as usual, after talking to either of his girls that, given their mother, it was amazing that they had turned out so well. He didn't discuss their mother with them unless they brought up the subject but he did know that they had next to no contact with her. What he also knew was that she liked to be thought of as a sort of sister to them; in other words, of the same generation; the poor deluded bitch. He almost ground his teeth.

Tiffany worked for a film company and her job was to source locations. She enjoyed this very much and, so far as he knew, she was pretty good at it. They had even used Laurel Park itself for films; it brought in some welcome extra income and the residents rather enjoyed the filming; occasionally some of them had even appeared as extras.

As he crossed the tennis court, he met Lady Moira walking with her 'companion,' Anna Louise. He liked Anna Louise very much and constantly wondered how she put up with Lady M. 'Afternoon, Ladies'.

'We're putting up the tennis netting, so perhaps we could have a game tomorrow, Anna Louise?'

'That would be lovely. By the way, my son, Matthew, is coming so perhaps we could get up a foursome? He's a bit lethal on the tennis court!'

'Goodness. Well, since neither of us has played during the winter, I suppose he'll wipe us out! Who shall we ask to make up a four? Janet?'

Janet was married to Reg Smyth and was also very good at tennis; her husband, on the other hand, was pretty useless although he didn't like to be left out. Not for the first time in the day, Peter reminded himself how hard it was to keep everyone happy. On the whole, he thought he didn't do badly but, inevitably, there were times when noses were put out of joint. One thing for certain, he could never do all the right things where Lady Moira was concerned and, frankly, he no longer really cared; she fancied herself too darn much. He had a secret laugh to himself when he remembered hearing her telling a new resident, someone who had just arrived, that she'd been born in a huge house, much larger than Laurel Park, and what a relief it had been to come to live somewhere smaller! The truth of the matter was, as Peter had found by complete chance, that her Mother had been a housemaid and her Father had worked in the stables at a stately home outside Birmingham; shock horror, they had never been married!! In a sneaky way, he thought he would only refer to the place of her birth if she really overstepped the line. One thing for sure, Lady M had managed to pick up some "posh" habits and "speak" that had lent some credence to her charade. She had been at Laurel Park for several years bullying her poor husband whom, Peter was certain, she had married entirely thanks to his title. This was only a Knighthood, but she loved calling herself 'Lady'. He could imagine that she had been very beautiful in her youth. Poor bloke, Ron had probably been seduced by her looks!

Chapter Three

He looked at his watch. God, he'd better get a move on and make sure the chairs were put in place for this evening. There were a number of people coming from the village who had bought their tickets online so he was estimating that there would be around sixty people, maybe a few more, this evening.

There were already rows of chairs set out in the Hall and Daisy, one of the housemaids, was dusting them off. 'Thanks, Daisy. Can we also get the bar set up, please. We only sell wine so we need just one size of glass but we'd better have a few tumblers for water.'

'Right you are, Mr Peter.' Daisy was a willing worker and he reminded himself constantly how fortunate he was in his staff.

The Hall was a very large room, rising through two stories, with a fine plasterwork ceiling dating from around the date that the house was built, 1580. Peter loved the room and he also loved holding events in it; it was what it had been made for! It was especially striking in the winter with the deep burgundy curtains drawn over the large Tudor windows and a fire burning in the enormous fireplace; the room looked huge but quite cosy, he always thought. Tonight, the curtains would not be closed as it probably wouldn't really be dark even by the end of the performance. He looked at the paintings on the walls. A collection of very fine Turners; he just wished he could have them all cleaned and generally spruced up but, right now he couldn't afford it. Conservation is a very pricey road but he swore to himself that he would deal with them just as soon as he could.

He looked around. Everything looked to be in order. 'Have the actors arrived yet?'

'Yes, I put them in the Library and sent them some coffee and those nice sticky buns Chef makes.'

'Well done, Daisy. I'll just go and say "Hello."'

He knocked on the Library door. It was opened by the woman who had been acting with the group for several years and who generally had a leading role. Lord, he'd forgotten her name; all he could think of was that it was unusual/exotic!

'Come in, come in!' she waved him into the room where her fellow thespians were sitting around in various stages of undress. The Library was a handsome room large but, at the same time, somehow quite cosy, too. Mahogany bookshelves lined the walls and several comfy, squishy looking leather upholstered sofas offered the reader a seat to retire to with their choice of reading matter and also provided a good spot for an afternoon snooze.

Dennis, leader of the group, who had had a couple of minor roles in the West End, in his youth, waved a languid hand, 'Hi Peter, here we are again! I hope your residents are all prepared for some blood and guts this evening!'

'Oh God, is it one of those? I think I saw it years ago in London and rather enjoyed it.'

'We'll do our best. It's very loosely based on that old chestnut: Dial M for Murder.'

'There are quite a number of people from the village coming so I think you'll have a good-size audience. Good luck!'

With a wave of his hand, he left the room and hearing the swish of gravel from outside the front door, he hurried to open it.

Tiffany had arrived accompanied by a swirl of wet air and a good waft of scent. 'Greetings, Dad, here I am,' she said.

'Wonderful, darling. I hope you're ready for the night's festivities? Shall I carry your bag upstairs?'

'No, no, I can still manage that, thanks all the same.' She vanished up the front stairs, calling back, 'I'll be down in a minute panting for a glass of something delicious!'

Chapter Four

Knowing that both his daughters had inherited his love of good wine, Peter walked through the Great Hall which lay ready for the evening's events, and into his pretty study at the other end of the South Front. He had a smallish refrigerator in a corner of the room which he kept, as he put it, stocked with the necessities of life. He hummed for a minute or two; what should it be. Ah yes, he pulled out a bottle of *Pol Roger*. As he twisted off the wire encircling the cork, he thought how fortunate it was that both the girls enjoyed nothing better than a glass of champagne; Jemima was in fact studying for her 'Master of Wine certificate'. She worked in London for a well-known wine company and she planned to become a specialist wine advisor either to a big company or to a restaurant chain. When she came to stay, she often brought a couple of unusual bottles for them to try together. He wondered if she planned to come this evening and almost as if it had been programmed, his phone burbled.

'Hi Dad. I'm on my way. See you soonest. Jem'.

'Well, that answers your question, Tiff. She's on her way.' He poured her a glass and they both watched, as if it was the first time they'd ever seen it, as the bubbles rose and fizzed gently before expiring.

'Never get tired of that sight!' Tiffany raised her glass to Peter, 'here's to us, Dad. May all go swimmingly this evening!'

'Amen!' Peter always got a little anxious before an event at the house. He so wanted everything to go "swimmingly" but was very aware that even the best laid plans could go awry. In truth, very few hiccups had occurred in his tenure as the owner of the house, but there was always a first time!

'Come on, he held his hand out to Tiffany, 'we must get some grub and be back before too many punters arrive.'

They walked back through the Great Room and down the stairs to the Dining Room where the clatter of cutlery on plates announced that supper was in full swing. A large sign at the entrance to the room announced the evening's entertainment and provided a reminder to many of the residents, who's memories were none too good, of what was in store after supper.

Peter had his own table at the back of the room which he found convenient as it enabled him to keep a watchful eye on most of the residents and he could take note of anyone who looked as if they needed more help. He was a kind man with a huge sense of humour that, as he often said, was an absolute essential in this job.

The room was pretty full already and it looked as if everyone was planning to come to see the play. Some had put on their 'party best' and the men were all in jacket and tie. Could be considered old-fashioned, thought Peter but he'd kept the rule of jackets in the dining room for supper and he felt, as he looked around, that older men definitely looked better whether they were fat or thin!

Supper was usually rather boarding school fare but it went down well with most of the residents. Tonight, the hot dish was "spag bog", which was always popular although Tiffany could never understand this. 'The problem is that it is something that can be reasonably good if it is "cooked to order" if you get my drift but, if it sits around for ages, it just goes into a clodgy mass. I can tell that it's popular because the serving dish is very nearly empty. I'm just going for the chocolate cake which looks fab and very naughty indeed!'

Peter hummed and hawed a bit before deciding to just have cheese which was always good. He served himself a large chunky of a runny camembert with the comment that 'I know I've taken a lot but it's really kindness to cheese because it's running away.'

'Of course it is, Dad, but I can see a raised eyebrow from your dearest resident. She probably wanted it herself but didn't want to risk it slipping off the plate. Shall I ask her?' Tiffany made as if to get up.

Peter laughed but put out a hand to stop her.

'Don't you dare!' They both giggled and Peter thought, for the umpteenth time, how fortunate he was to have his daughters.

'Come on' he said a few moments later,' let's go and secure some good seats.

They left the dining room having exchanged brief chitchat with most of the residents who were still polishing off their supper, urging them to come and see the play.

Chapter Five

The big front door was now standing open and some dozen members of the public were already taking their seats. 'Looks as if it is going to be popular, which is good. Come on let's sit at the back.' Peter was smiling and shaking hands with various members of the public. People continued to pour in, some realising that they had a few minutes in hand before "curtain up," bought themselves a glass of wine from the Bar which was manned by Daisy and Julia, another member of the staff. Peter's theory was that the prettier the servers, the more they, the punters, were likely to buy!

'Good grief,' exclaimed Peter, counting the very few empty seats, 'I think I'd better see if I can find a few more chairs.' Seeing a couple who were plainly searching for empty seats, he got up and, taking Tiffany by the hand, pulled her with him, 'Here, Sir take these.'

A bell was rung from the stage, 'Five minutes to curtain.'

Peter opened a cupboard in the Hall and revealed at least a dozen more chairs. Seeing Sam, his new assistant groundsman, he waved to him to come and help. 'Thanks, Sam. We've got a huge audience this evening.' It was true, there were now at least one hundred plus people in the Hall. It was more than their plays usually drew which was generally around the fifty mark. 'I thought people might be bored of murder but, evidently I was wrong!'

It took a few more minutes for the late comers to get seated and there was a general hubble bubble of conversation before three loud 'thumps' on the stage floor heralded the start of the play.

The set was a large sitting room comfortably furnished with armchairs and sofas, the usual upper middleclass sort of room, thought Peter. There were also two doors. Having surrendered his chair, he was leaning against the bar from which vantage point, he could see right across the stage. Tiff had found a stool and was perching beside him. She whispered to him that she thought she had just heard Jemima arriving.

'I'll go and see.' Peter walked back into the entrance hall. Jemima was already halfway up the first flight of the stairs. She waved and called, 'I'll be right down. '

The events on stage were now well under way with the male and female leads at each other's throats; Tiffany squeezed her father's hand and raised her eyebrows: 'familiar'? she said.

He rolled his eyes. 'I'd rather forget it.' It was true, he'd hated the endless vicious rows with his former wife but it was somehow difficult to explain his feelings nowadays to his children. He'd forgotten the details of the play's various plots but now found it almost too near the truth to be funny; Margot the lead was having an affair with an American. Tony, her husband, discovers this and plots to bump off the woman. He decides to enlist the services of a criminal friend, Lesgate. (How many of us have criminal friends conveniently to hand?) and just as things were really warming up....the interval arrived.

'God, I need a strong drink. Let's go to the study and I'll find something stiffer than a glass of cheap, well cheapish, white wine.' Peter led the way across the hall which was still fairly full of members of the audience who didn't want to fight their way to the Bar.

Once in his study, he excavated a bottle of Scotch and three glasses from a cupboard behind the desk. 'My secret cache!'

'I bet you need it quite often if you've been ambushed by Lady M,' laughed Jemma. Jemma is the younger of his two daughters and resembles her mother in her good looks although, as Peter has pointed out once or twice, fortunately not in any other respect.

'It's so good to have you both here. Are you enjoying the play?' Peter always wanted feedback even if his children were a generation or two younger than most of the audience and were, therefore, likely to have slightly different tastes!

'So far,' Tiffany was hedging her bets, 'but it is ideal, cast-wise etc. for this type of venue, isn't it? The burning question being, "who is going to be bumped off?"'

Jemima had now joined them explaining that her boyfriend was so tired that he was having a quick nap. She picked some sheets of paper off Peter's desk, 'Now let's each write down the name of our suspected victim and that of the murderer?'

Jem then folded each sheet of paper and put them under the blotter on the desk.

'Well, I know whom I would kill off!' her father said, 'but that might refer to a member of the audience.'

They all laughed when the bell rang for the second act.

Just as they were taking up their station in the doorway from the bar, a scream, a piercing scream sounded followed by noise that sounded like furniture being chucked about.

'Good God, Peter leaped up and rushed to the bar. Nothing there; he left the area which formed the stage; where the fuck were the actors? He rushed across the 'stage' and yanked open one of the two doors on the far side. As he pulled the first door wide open, a body fell to the floor in front of him. He froze for an instant before dropping to the floor and pulling the body over: it was a youngish man. All Peter could think of was that it was a member of the cast. 'Ring 999', he shouted at Jemima.

He was aware of a crowd of people pressing forward to get a look. 'Get back, get back and sit down, please. AT ONCE!' He felt the young man's neck for sign of a pulse; a flutter gave him hope but it died away and looking at the face of the body, Peter knew it was too late. He closed the eyelids realising that the man was actually not as young as he had thought. Was this the man who was playing the role of the American lover in the play?

'Tiff and Jem, you two get everyone back into the hall and sitting down and, quick as you can, make sure that nobody leaves the house.'

Somewhere a door slammed shut. 'Where the fuck was that? Quick did somebody leave the house?'

Another piercing scream; oh dear God thought Peter, this is turning into a nightmare.

He got up and yanked open the other door on the far side of the room. He came face to face with Hazel, the maid. 'What is it, Hazel, have you seen something? The girl threw herself at him, sobbing. He had difficulty untangling what she said since she was completely hysterical. Finally, he slapped her face (not too hard) 'what have you seen, Hazel? Just calm down and tell me.'

The girl shuddered but her sobs slowly subsided, 'he had a big knife, I think he went out of the window.' She gulped before continuing 'he waved it at me, the knife I mean, and shouted, 'Shut up you cow, or you'll be next!'

'I just screamed,' I think.

Peter tried to stay calm, 'which window did he go out of, Hazel?

'The one at the far end of the front hall. It was wide open you see because it was so stuffy,' she sniffed.

Peter rushed out of the room and across the hall; the lower sash of the window was pushed up. He looked out and saw footprints in the flower bed. As he debated with himself as to what he should do next, the sound of a police siren on blue lights pierced the air. Two cars roared up the drive and came to a halt with a swirl of gravel; even as he felt a great relief, he also couldn't help thinking that Higgins would be livid at the desecration of the gravel sweep in front of the house. (How does it happen that, in moments of panic, pure trivia often pokes its nose in?)

Chapter Six

Peter opened the huge front door. There were two police officers on the doorstep, 'You've had an incident, Sir?'

'An incident?' Peter tried to collect his wits. "An incident" made it sound so trivial. 'Yes, yes, come in, come in. Follow me.'

He led the way into the Great Room where most of the audience were still sitting and through to the bar area. 'He indicated the body lying in the doorway. 'I'm afraid he's dead; I just turned him over otherwise I haven't touched him.'

'OK, Sir, let's have a look'. A minute later, he looked up and shook his head. 'I'm afraid you're right, Sir. I'll ring for an ambulance to come and pick him up. How long ago did this happen? Could we sit down and, I'm afraid, as you can imagine, we will have a lot of questions.'

Peter looked at the body. There was now a huge pool of blood from the man's chest and neck although the face was very pale but remarkably peaceful. 'I have seen several dead bodies and am always amazed at their faces; seldom troubled even by the brutality of death; it is really as if their soul has left the body in peace.'

The lead policeman smiled saying, 'Yes, I know what you mean. Our photographer will come and take some pictures.

Now, Sir come and sit down and answer some questions, please.'

'Before we start on that, perhaps you should take a look out of the window in the entrance hall. That is how the man escaped and when I looked out of the window, I could see some footprints in the flowerbed.'

It didn't take but a minute for the police to verify this but when the policeman returned from checking, he looked a bit concerned. 'Yes, you are quite right, Sir but we've found a second body in the Library.'

'The Library?' Peter sounded as if he'd never heard of such a place. He sat down in the chair by his desk with something of a thump. 'What d'you mean? A body in the Library? I mean the cast was using the Library.'

'Sorry, Sir but it was behind that big leather sofa.'

'Black leather sofa?' Peter knew he was babbling but, somehow, he couldn't grasp what the policemen was saying. Who is it?'

'A lady, Sir.'

'A lady?' Peter knew he was sounding ever increasingly demented as he repeated everything the policemen said, but, somehow, he couldn't really relate to what the man was telling him.

'Perhaps, if you wouldn't mind, you could come and identify her for us?'

'I must?' he mumbled.

'Please, Sir, it won't take but a minute and would be a great help to us.'

Peter followed the detective out of the room, across the broad passage and into the Library, passing a constable who was patently keeping guard on the door. He smiled wanly at the man as he passed him.

The Library was a mess. The term "dressing room" sprang to Peter's mind as he looked around. He mumbled something about "dressing room" and the detective said 'yes, Sir, I understand that this was where the cast changed and made-up.'

There were clothes everywhere and an unbidden, unconnected thought sprang to Peter's mind, *"do they live like this at home?"*

The detective beckoned him over, 'here we are, could you have a good look and tell me if you can identify the body.'

He drew a deep breath and followed the policeman across the room.

There behind the big sofa, a body lay stretched out. The person was on her back and her skirt was ruffled up round her waist exposing skinny legs and a pair of M and S beige briefs. Her head was turned to one side but there was no mistaking who it was: Lady M. Peter let out a deep breath. Why one earth would anyone murder the old woman, maddening though she was.

'Yes, Inspector, its Lady Moira Colquhound, a resident here.' Peter pronounced her surname "Cohoun" and felt the old woman would be nodding her approval; despite her real antecedents, the old bird is, he corrected himself, "was" a crashing snob.

'How was she killed? There's a lot of blood round her head.'

'Well, we need forensics to check but I think it could have been with that same knife. We need to find it. My men are going to be searching everywhere inside and out, could you inform your guests and the residents please.

'Of course. When can the audience leave?'

'I'll have my men make a list of names and addresses and then most of them may go. We can contact them later as needed.'

Peter felt a hand slip into his own and gave it a squeeze; it was Tiffany. 'OK Dad?'

'Oh darling, I feel completely flattened. I don't know who the dead guy in the doorway by the bar is, but, as you can see, this is Lady M. What she was doing in here in the middle of a performance, I have absolutely no idea. It's going to be a long night, darling. Before anything else, I must find poor old Ron. Hard to know how he will take it.'

Chapter Seven

They retreated to the study where Peter slumped down in his desk chair. 'Darling Tiff, be an angel and get us a glass from my secret cache. I am just flummoxed; don't know what to do or what to think.

A knock on the door and the police Inspector, name of Carstairs, came in. 'Could I possibly use this room for interviews, please?'

Feeling rather hounded on all sides and dreading the effect the news of the two deaths would have on the rest of the residents, he said, 'Of course.' He put out his hand to TIffany and said, 'come on, darling, let's go to the Drawing room but first, I must tell the residents what has happened; no hysterics, I hope.'

'Wouldn't count on that! I bet Primrose flips and needs smelling salts.'

They walked into the Great Hall where there was a roaring level of conversation; as Peter walked through to the far side of the room, he heard snippets of what was being said, swirling around. Needless to say, most of it was highly inaccurate but one thing stood out: Lady Moira. It would seem that she had stabbed a member of the cast, no not one, but two members of the cast! God, how rumours flew, thought Peter as the picture of Lady M stabbing the man (who had just been identified as the bloke who played the American in the play) leaped before his eyes. He blinked rapidly to get rid of this unwelcome interference, and clapping his hands and putting on his parade ground voice, he asked for quiet.

The room fell silent quite swiftly.

'Thank you everyone. Now I can tell from snippets of conversation that I have just heard as I walked through the room, you are pretty much all aware that an event of considerable seriousness has occurred.'

'The truth of this is that two people have lost their lives; both apparently murdered. One is a man who was one of the actors, John Long, the other was one of our own, a resident, Lady Moira.' As he paused for breath and to make real impact, a huge crescendo of noise rose from the sixty or so people still in the room.

To put an end to the wild speculation which was rapidly taking an even firmer hold of the crowded room, he clapped again and called for silence. 'Perhaps it would be suitable if we have a moment of quiet before I continue. Let us reflect for a moment or two on the two lives which have been lost in acts of violence.' The room fell silent.

He became aware of something happening at the other side of the room; yes, it was, indeed, Primrose. Catching sight of Georges and Hazel standing quite near to the door leading to the front hall, he indicated to them that they should remove her. Georges raised his hand in acknowledgement and between himself and the maid, they managed to remove the hysterical woman.

Peter continued, 'The police would like to have the names and addresses of all non-residents. If you think that you might have helpful information, they may require you to stay and make a statement. All others will be permitted to leave. Whilst you are waiting to give the police the information that they want, I should like to offer you all a glass of wine. I hope this sad event will not prevent you all from coming to further events at Laurel Park.'

Peter was well liked in the local community and the audience crowded around him to commiserate and wish him well.

The sound of corks being drawn announced the arrival of the wine and the heavy atmosphere lightened a trifle.

'Well done, Dad.' Jemima gave him a hug, 'very well done.'

'Who on earth would do these terrible things; who and why? There's no sense in stabbing an old woman to death'; he paused, 'unless she saw something, of course. I suppose that must have been it.'

They reached the study and deciding that events warranted something a bit more powerful than a glass of wine, Peter pulled out a fine bottle of a single malt saying, 'well this should perk us up!'

He poured them each a shot and then groaned. 'Oh God! I'll have to talk to the guy who is in charge of the actors.' He stopped for a moment 'you two do realise that the man killed was one of his Company?'

'Had you met him before?' asked Tiffany.

'Not that I can remember but you know, I didn't really look at his face, I was just too appalled by all the blood.'

'Did Lady M bleed much?' asked Tiffany. 'I never would have credited her with any blood; she aways seemed such a cold fish!'

'Now for heaven's sake, Tiff, don't talk like that, she was a human being for all her faults.' Jemima was a bit shocked by her sister although, deep down, she did understand where Tiff was coming from.

They sipped their Scotch in silence for a few minutes. Peter was busy thinking of all the things he had to do such as informing Lady M's family, helping Ron to arrange her funeral, calming hysterical residents and getting all the bloodstains cleaned up just for starters.

Peter swallowed the rest of his drink in one gulp and got up. 'I think I must see to the residents and talk to the actors; see you later.'

The previous hubbub in the Great Hall had died down with the departure of most of the outsiders and pinning on a smile, Peter walked through the room full of residents, exchanging a few words with some of them. In answer to the question on everyone's lips, he had to say that he did not know anything, as yet. 'Frankly, I suggest that everyone heads off to bed now and let the police do what they have to do.'

Having assured himself that, apart from Primrose, everyone was fairly calm, Peter left the Hall and went to the Library. Here he found a heavy silence. Dennis got up from his position, stretched out on the sofa, and shook Peter by the hand. 'I don't know what has happened to young John Long. You know the guy who plays the American lover; he's vanished. I haven't told the Inspector as yet because I assumed he'd gone for a pee or something but I am a bit concerned. I don't suppose you've seen him have you, Peter?'

Peter shook his head. Turning to the other members of the cast, 'you all OK?' They all nodded. 'Do any of you know where John has gone?'

Again, they all shook their heads. The only woman involved, 'It's all very peculiar. I was the only person who was meant to be murdered and we just never got to that moment in the play.' She sounded whiny as if she'd been done some sort of injustice. 'I can't think where John has gone; he should have told me.'

Peter wondered about this; were the two an item? He turned to Dennis raising an eyebrow in a query.

The actor was looking very surprised but he just shook his head and shrugged.

Peter struggled to recall John. He hadn't had a chance to get to know this new member of the cast.

Dennis sensing Peter's problem, 'Yes, John is new to our group but Philly had met him and thought he would be a good addition so we are putting him in a couple of plays and seeing how he gets on. This is the first we've done with him.'

All Peter could think of was that he must be Ophelia's newest "toy boy" but he just said, enigmatically, 'I see.'

'Well, I don't! Dennis snapped.' I told you, Ophelia, that I wouldn't have any more of your lovers in the group. It simply never works out, and you promised me that he was just someone you had met by chance.'

Ophelia made a sort of *moue*. I'm sorry Den but I can't help it if someone is attracted to me.'

'Oh, for Christ's sake, Philly, grow up. 'Den barked.

Peter hid a smile behind his hand, were all actresses so vain? 'You won't be able to put on M for Murder, will you? Not enough cast members.'

'You're right. Even trying to double up just wouldn't work, would it. If we're not careful, we'll be down to monologues! Den laughed drily.' Seriously, where has that man got to?'

'Do you know if he had any acquaintances around here?'

'Naw, doubt it and, anyhow, surely he wouldn't have gone visiting in the middle of the play!' Dennis stood up and peeled off his shirt and then, realising he was not yet finished for the day, put it back on. 'It's bedtime for me after I've spoken to the cops, all this has really worn me out with worry etc. Where the fuck has that bloody boy got to?'

A knock at the door and the Inspector put his head in, 'Could you come and have a talk with me now, Sir,' he said to Dennis. He added, 'We've found the young man, I think.'

'I'll ring his bloody neck when I catch up with him,' growled Dennis.

Well Sir, I think someone else has already had the same idea. Come with me please.

Chapter Eight

Peter eventually crawled into his magnificent four poster at around 2am. The house was still full of policemen and forensics specialists but he was so exhausted that he simply had to lie down and the Inspector told him he'd be more help in the morning if he'd had some sleep.

Sleep! If only! Events of the last few hours swirled through his mind. Two people killed in the house in the space of about five minutes and then, a guy missing. It didn't bear thinking about except that he had to. His last call before coming to bed had been to talk to Ron. He had not quite known what to expect from this. He knew, only too well that the poor man had been mercilessly bullied by his wife, Lady Moira, and, frankly, if the murderer had been Ron, he would have almost understood; a case of the worm turns.

He'd run Ron to ground in the Great Hall. The poor fellow was sitting surrounded by 'well-wishers', ie other residents. He visibly brightened up when he saw Peter and the latter swept away all the others with a 'Let's leave poor Ron alone, right now, he's a lot to think about.'

Ron was looking quite bemused and all he could say was, 'Is it really true? I mean I know it must be but it's hard to take in.'

'I know, it is, of course it is. All I can think of right now is that she was killed in error; that the target was someone else and she somehow got in the way. So very sorry, Ron.'

'Don't think it's really sunk in so far, Peter. I just feel sort of empty. I think I'll go to bed and see if it's all been a bad dream in the morning. '

'A good idea, Ron. Peter escorted him to the stairs and clapping him on the should said, 'take one of Her Ladyship's renowned sleeping tablets and get some rest.'

Now, as he lay back in bed and went over the events of the evening, Peter thought once again of the actor who had vanished. He tried to recall the youngish man, John Long, who was missing and, therefore, inevitably, a likely subject as the perpetrator until he could be found and accused or otherwise. It was pretty extraordinary, if he was innocent, that he had vanished just as he was to open in his role in the play; his first role with the Company. Medium height, quite goodlooking was all Peter could summon up. Must ask the girls, he thought, just as sheer exhaustion took him off.

Chapter Nine

The sun was creeping across the room when Peter became fully awake some four hours later. He was just thinking that he might stay in bed for another hour or two, when the events of the previous evening rushed into his mind and the notion of a "lie-in" was instantly banished. God! Poor old Ron. He wondered if the man had managed to get some rest.

He got dressed in a dark suit and scrabbled in his tie drawer for a black one. *One doesn't wear them very often,* he mused, as he knotted it round his neck. What should he do first? Well, a cup of strong coffee would possibly kick-start his brain, he felt he was going to have to be on the ball today.

Reaching the dining room, he was relieved to find that he was the first; he hated the small talk that always ensued when one met some of the residents at the breakfast table.

He checked the time, 7.45. Yes, well, he was early but fortunately a big jug of coffee sat on the hotplate accompanied by some hot milk. He carried his mug to the window and stood sipping cautiously. The big window looked out over a huge herbaceous border with paeonies, roses and lupins all jockeying for attention; it was a pleasing sight. The only conclusion he had come to was that Lady Moira had been killed by mistake. Of course, he would often have loved to wring her skinny neck when she was being especially tiresome and demanding BUT for somebody to actually stab her to death, well that was not really credible, not here, not in Laurel Place.

His thoughts then turned to his younger daughter, Jemima. The evening before, he'd only caught a glimpse of the young man she had brought; he just hoped neither of the girls would make the same mistake as he had in who they eventually married. "Suitable" was often the expression used when describing a *fiancé* but he knew the sort of man he hoped they would find; no hurry! After throwing his wife out he had spent endless nights tossing and turning wondering if he had deprived his daughters of their mother but it never took long for him for him to dismiss the idea; he never wanted to see the bitch again and, in fact, neither did they! Unnatural, he sometimes told himself but, on the other hand, how did you "manufacture" real love between family members if it didn't exist? He knew that Kathy, one of the residents, would tell him, in shocked tones, should he express the problem to her, and in her practising Christian mode, that God tells us that we love our children unconditionally, sort of automatically. Hmm.

He tossed off the remains of his coffee just as Jem came in followed by her boyfriend. 'Dad, this is Luke. Sorry I didn't tell you he was coming but he was/is scared of meeting you and last night he went straight to sleep.'

Peter held out his hand to Luke, who shook it saying "Luke Hervey, Sir".

'I'm sure Jem will have told you that we are having a spot of trouble here: namely two murders so you must forgive me if I seem a bit distracted. Help yourself to breakfast, I'm off to see what the Inspector is doing.'

He found the Inspector in the kitchen speaking in fluent French to Georges.

Peter greeted Georges, saying, 'Now you can see that not all the English are savages, some of us even speak French.'

Georges roared with laughter saying, *'Oui et ce monsieur, il parle tres bien!'*

The policeman smiled, 'thank you Georges. And I'd love another of those scrumptious looking *brioches*.'

They all laughed but, of course, the chef was very chuffed that this senior policeman loved his food.

'Now, Georges don't go getting above yourself, 'laughed Peter, 'I just wanted to let you know that Jemima has brought a friend with her,' here Jem raised a hand to Georges So it will be another mouth to feed for lunch.

'Inspector, I think you met the young man briefly last night.'

'Don't think so, but whatever, I'll need to speak with him, perhaps this afternoon so don't let him slip off.'

Peter was in fact quite annoyed with Jemima; what a moment she'd chosen to bring a stranger home but he decided that instituting a row at this moment was not likely to be a good idea.' I didn't know she was bringing him,' he said to the policeman, 'Daughters you know!' He turned to Georges 'You can only eat like a mouse because we are always short of food, *n'est ce pas*, Georges!'

Georges chuckled, not rising to the bait. He looked out of the kitchen window that opened onto the back yard, he pointed as he looked at Peter who nodded and indicated to the Inspector. There were two black vans pulling up outside.

The Inspector nodded saying 'yes, the bodies are being taken to the morgue in Maidstone. A proper PM will be done there; Dr Khan is expecting them. I've told him that I need the results ASAP. I think I should now see the husband first.'

Peter went off, together with the Inspector, to go and find poor Ron whom they finally discovered sitting in the dining room table, hands clasped around a mug, staring at nothing. He was ashen in colour and looking very nervous. Peter patted him on the shoulder feeling totally inadequate, 'So sorry about this old man. Anything I can help you do? This is the policeman who's investigating Moira's death.'

Ron replied to all the policeman's questions saying he had absolutely no idea why someone would murder his wife. 'Yes, she was bossy and opinionated but that isn't sufficient reason, is it?'

Sometime later, the Inspector was writing up a note when his phone rang. 'Yes, who is it?'

'Dr Khan here. I thought I should let you know as soon as possible that the woman was not murdered. I think and am pretty certain, that she had a massive heart attack perhaps brought on by shock, and then fell hitting her head very hard on the corner of something such as a cabinet, and then landing on the ground. She moreoreless eventually bled to death. Heads, as I'm sure you know, do bleed a great deal and on top of the heart attack…'

Silence

'Good God, so she wasn't murdered at all?
'Apparently not.'

Another long silence which Peter noted, the Inspector did not make any effort to break.

Eventually, Ron in a rather shaky voice, 'it really comes to the same thing, doesn't it? She's dead!'

'I'm afraid so, Sir. Did she have any history of heart disease?'

Ron shook his head, 'Not so far as I knew.'

Peter then asked rather tentatively about the man who had died. Of course, he was wondering if it could be the guy who had gone missing from the actors' group. As if he could read Peter's thoughts, there was a knock on the door and Dennis came in.

'Is it OK if I come in?' he asked rather tentatively.

The Inspector looked at him for a moment and then waved him to a chair. He then picked up a folder and pulled out a large colour photo, 'Do you know this man?' he asked.

Dennis took the photo. A quick glance and he gulped; it was not a pretty sight. 'Yes', he dropped the photo and raced out of the room. A heavy silence was eventually broken by a knock on the door and a young policeman put his head round it, 'gent upchucking in the cloakroom, Sir.'

'Well!' Peter looked pale even though he had not seen the photo yet. He was quite easily rendered queasy. 'It would seem that I was lucky not to be shown that photo.'

'Sometimes', said the Inspector, 'you can get a good reaction by sort of "blind-siding" a witness or suspect.'

'I see', said Peter, although he was not quite sure that he did. 'Poor old Dennis. I hope you don't show it to Ophelia, you know Dennis' leading lady.'

'Why d'you think it would shock her?'

'Well, women aren't usually keen on blood and gore, are they? I know my daughters won't go to horror films.'

The Inspector laughed saying 'my sixteen year old son thinks the gorier the better.'

'That's boys for you! Any news yet?' Not unnaturally Peter was very anxious that the murderer should be caught as soon as possible.'

'No! not yet but I should like to speak to anyone who saw your missing actor pm yesterday. It's hard to think who would have known that actor was here. You know, he'd only just joined the company and this was his first appearance.

Peter suddenly realised he might need his wallet which he had somehow left upstairs in his bedroom and left the Inspector starting to speak with one resident after another.

When he turned into the Picture Gallery on the first floor, he saw someone vanishing at the far end. Running down the long room shouting 'Hullo, who is that, who is there'; he felt a bit silly when he turned the corner and found Hazel, a very long feather duster in hand, trying to trap a spider's web hanging on tightly rather high up.

'Did someone just go through here?' he asked her.

The girl laughed, 'he was going too fast for me to do more than tell him to slow down, "Sir!", and to 'watch out where he was going.'

'Did he answer you?'

'No, he just vanished.'

Peter stood still as he wondered who it had been and why he was in such a hurry.

Suddenly, a loud shout and one of the young policemen came racing up the stairs, 'Sir, Sir!'

'You want me or your Boss?'

The panting copper, 'there's been a robbery.'

The Inspector who had been following Peter to the first floor, 'Calm down, Smithers, calm down and tell me what has happened.'

'Yes, Sir, the old lady.' The young man stopped to take a breath, 'You knows the old lady wot died?'

'Of course. 'He saw Ron coming slowly up the stairs, 'You OK Ron?'

The poor fellow appeared utterly distraught. Peter pushed him down into a convenient chair, 'now slow down Ron and take some deep breaths, in through the nose.'

Tiffany was suddenly beside him so Peter grasped her hand, 'I'm waiting for Ron to catch his breath and tell us what has happened.'

Ron, still in an obvious state of shock. 'Moira's jewellery,' he mumbled, 'it's gone!'

'Moira's jewellery is gone,' Peter parroted as he tried to digest what Ron was saying.

The elderly man, looking frailer by the minute, 'Yes, it's all gone,' he laughed hysterically, 'but she's dead, isn't she? She's gone!' He was now sobbing quietly.

Peter exchanged looks with the Inspector, 'Tiff, you stay with Ron, OK. I'm just going to his apartment.

The Inspector and Peter were almost running as they took off down the Gallery where Hazel was still standing, mouth open, feather duster still gripped in her hand.

'Be a kind girl and help Tiff with Sir Ronald, please.'

They reached Ronald's apartment which lay down a long corridor on the opposite side of the house and the two men reached the door puzzled rather than nervous. Ron had left the door open; they found Anna Louise standing in the doorway.

'What on earth is going on?' she asked.

'Have you been inside?

'No, I just got here after hearing all the racket!'

The Inspector pushed the door wide with a gloved hand. 'Don't touch anything, anything at all.'

Followed closely by Peter, the Inspector headed down the passage towards the back of the apartment. They passed the sitting room which appeared untouched, another room which looked like a man's dressing room, and on to the far end of the apartment. Here was a large room with a huge fourposter bed and several deep cupboards; one of these stood, its doors ajar.

Inside was a large very solid looking safe. It appeared to be closed but when the Inspector pulled the knob, it swung open.

'How did you open it, Sir?' he asked Ronald, who had caught up with them.

'Like you, I pulled it and found it was unlocked.'

'When was that?'

'This morning. I seldom open it but I wanted some cufflinks that I don't wear very often. Obviously, I was horrified when I found the safe was empty, well not empty but all the boxes are empty.'

'When exactly was this?'

'Around 9am.'

'Can you describe, Sir, what is missing?'

'I can describe, loosely, some of the best or most pricey items but, to tell you the truth, I'm not very interested in jewellery. It was my wife who bought it all.'

'Valuable?'

'Some of it, yes; very!'

'So, who else might know what was in it?'

'Frankly, I don't have any idea but I would suspect my wife may have discussed it with some of the women who live here. You know, women are usually more interested in such things.'

The Inspector called two of his team and told them to dust the safe and all around it, for prints.' He looked at Peter and shrugged his shoulder, 'that's all we can do for the moment.'

'We'll get the prints and see if anything matches – not very optimistic about any of the residents but we'll see. I'm prepared to be astounded! In this job you must always keep an open mind. Your daughters are both here, I think?'

'Yes, they came for the play.'

Peter had a niggling feeling, for an unknown reason, that he should find out more about Jem's boyfriend before discussing him with the police. Was he withholding evidence?

He added, 'I doubt very much that they would have known anything about Lady M's jewellery.'

'No, I don't expect they do but keep your ears pinned open. Someone knows something.' He went off down the stairs leaving two of his men to get on with the fingerprinting.

Peter met Jemima plus boyfriend on his way to the study. 'Have you been interviewed yet?' he asked his daughter.

'Not yet. They want to see Luke, too, although I told them he was asleep upstairs last night, they still need to clear him.'

At that moment a young policeman came out of the study tapped Luke on the should saying, 'the Inspector will see you now.'

Jemima made to go with him but was politely told to wait where she was.

In the Study, the Inspector waved Luke to a chair as his own phone rumbled. 'Yes? You've found what? He listened some more before picking up a pen and scribbling some numbers on a pad lying on the desk. 'Thanks, see if you can get some prints off the paper you've found.' He got up saying to Luke, 'Sorry, I'll have to come back to you. Wait please.'

As soon as the policeman left the room, Luke stood up and as he passed Jemima, he said, 'Sorry, babe, must have a pee.' He left the room.

Peter looked around, no Tiff. 'Tiff still in bed, Jem?'

'Yes, she was just finishing a book and said she would be down as soon as she had, but then on the way Dad nobbled her to look after poor Sir Ron. Oh Bijou, you beast!'

This was addressed to the golden retriever who, still wet from her morning swim, had shaken herself violently sending spray in all directions.

'Oh great, Hazel. The maid had come in wielding a large rough dog towel. She also grabbed the black labrador retriever, Lucifer, and rubbed him firmly. The instant she released him, he made for the rug in front of the fireplace and rolled ecstatically, over and over as if relieving the worst itch in the world.

'Thanks so much Hazel. I don't know where Luke has gone; he said he was going for a pee.'

'Oh, your friend? He went out through the kitchen ages ago.'

'Out?'

'I'm pretty sure it was him—about ten minutes ago.'

Jemima frowned and talking pretty much to herself, said, ' I wonder where on earth he has gone?'

Chapter Ten

Meanwhile up in Lady Moira's apartment, the Inspector had been shown the piece of paper with the six digits, preceded by a star, written on it, which had been found in the dead man's pocket.

'You've got the prints off this?' he asked, holding the plastic envelope by one corner.

'Yes, Sir, I think we may have a match. We're just checking.'

'You know what this is don't you?'

'Yes, Sir. And we do think we have a match. Just triple checking to be sure. D'you want us to close the safe, Sir?' The men walked back into Lady Moira's bedroom.

'Yes, I want to give these numbers a go – I'm pretty sure they make up the code for opening it. The Inspector briefly closed his eyes and then kneeling in front of the big safe, entered the code as written on the paper preceded by a star.

"click" and the door was open.

'Well done, Sir!', the young detective was impressed.

Inside there was a large collection of velvet covered jewellery boxes but just as he put his hand out to pick up the first box, something glittery on the floor caught his eye. He bent to pick it up before drawing back, 'Take a photo, Jennings'. A flash!

'Done, Sir. Do you think there has been a robbery?'

'Looks probable. Go and find Sir Ronald and ask him politely if he could come here.

'Now,' addressing the other young policeman, 'put on gloves and then take all these boxes out, one by one, printing them as you go and put them in rows on this table, he indicated a fabulous Georgian side table with walnut and mother of pearl inlay; wait a moment and I'll get something to protect this beautiful work. So saying, he picked a pillow off the bed and pulled off its cover, followed by a second one and, due to the number of boxes a third. 'Once you have them all out and dusted for prints, we shall open them and film it. I think some people may be going to be surprised.'

Peter and Jemima had caught up with Tiffany and Ron and now they all arrived in the apartment together.

'What's the matter, what on earth is going on?' demanded Ron.

'Someone has stolen a lot of your wife's jewellery.' He pointed to the line of expensive boxes sitting on the table.

'Most of them are empty. Whoever has stolen the other bits, certainly knew what he was taking. I don't suppose you recall the last time you opened the safe?'

Ron scratched his chin, 'No, not really. Sorry.'

The detective pulled the object he had found on the floor, from his pocket. 'What about this?'

'Oh, my goodness!' Ron suddenly became quite animated. 'Of course! 'I remember that piece. It is one of the few bits that I bought for her as opposed to her choosing things for herself. I think I paid about £12,000 for it and that would have been around twenty years ago when we got married.'

'Please have a good look amongst both your papers and her's, of course, in case she made any sort of catalogue. If you find anything, please bring it to me at once.'

Ron mumbled, 'yes, I'll do that right away.'

'Next', the Inspector sounded quite fierce, 'I must speak to Mr Hervey. He came here with you?' he nodded to Jemima 'but I'm very much afraid he has run off with the jewellery. This is a serious matter.'

Poor Jemima blanched visibly. She stammered, 'I had absolutely no idea. 'She held up her phone, he's not picking up!'

The Inspector, who would have been even more surprised if he had done so, 'give me the phone please.' He now grilled poor Jemima as to how when and where she had met Luke. Did she know how he made a living, apart from robbery? It had been noted that he wore expensive clothes. Did she know where he had come from. Jemima was in tears by this time as she said she had met him at a big party in London several months earlier.

The Inspector patted her shoulder, 'Thank you Miss Jemima. That'll be all for now, but we shall probably come back to you so please do not leave Laurel Place. You must also write out a statement for me. Jennings will sort that out with you. OK?'

Jemima was drying her tears with Peter's silk handkerchief, 'I think I've been a bloody, naïve fool.'

'Don't beat yourself up over it, darling,' Peter felt very concerned about her, 'There's no way you could have known he was a criminal.' Peter would happily have wrung the man's neck. He was also wondering how he had left the house since he had arrived with Jem in her car.

The Policeman's thoughts were on the same track, it would seem; 'go and see if anyone in the kitchen or in the yard behind the house, saw him actually leave; perhaps he hitched a life with a tradesman or delivery driver. You must a have lots of them rolling in and out every day, Sir?'

'Yes, course we do.' Peter looked out of the window which overlooked the back courtyard.' Where did you leave your car, Jem?'

'Oh God, isn't it there?' she paused. 'D'you think he's nicked it? Bastard!'

Peter called to the policeman guarding the front door to the apartment. Tell your Boss that it appears he has also helped himself to Jemima's car!'

They went down the handsome front stairs which Jem generally couldn't help admiring each time she went up and down but this time, the beautifully curved wood of the rail and the complicated twisted spindles, went quite unnoticed.

Residents had been asked to keep to their rooms for the time being so as not to hamper the police's investigations, and, thus the Hall seemed temporarily very quiet. They crossed the large empty space, all the bits and pieces of furniture for the play, having been removed.

They found the Inspector sitting in the study and Jem told him of the theft of her car.

'Reg number? She was in such a state by now that it took a few minutes before she could remember it. Her pretty face was stained by tears.

'That's OK, Miss, your Dad remembered it. I suppose the thief took the key from your room?'

'Yes, I must have left it on the dressing table,' she gulped. I just can't believe he's done this to me.'

Tiffany who had been seduced by the glamour of the jewellery came running in, 'I just heard about your car Jem. I'm so terribly sorry. She looked at the policeman? Is there really nothing we can do?'

'Not right now. Don't worry, we'll get him but we've got to pick him up first. Now I've got to have a word with the actor man. I think he's in the library; could you show me the way, please.' He turned to Jemima, 'we'll let you know the moment we have news but I have to tell you that whoever took it, then his prints match those on the boxes.'

The two girls looked at each other and groaned.

'You mean that whoever stole the jewellery also stole the car?'

'Greedy bugger!' Tiff was astonished.

Arriving at the Library, the door was opened by Ophelia who ushered them in with her most engaging smile, 'Come on in, I think Dennis is waiting for you.

Dennis himself was quite bewildered, 'What the fuck is going on? My fingerprints have been taken plus a mug shot and I was told that none of us could leave yet.' He sounded very indignant. 'I understand that John's been killed but I hardly knew the guy, he had only just joined my Company and, Goddamit, on the very first night, he was killed. God knows who killed him, but it certainly wasn't I!'

The Inspector using his most friendly voice, 'I'm sure you can understand, Sir, we have to slowly eliminate people; it takes time. Do you happen to know if he had any acquaintance in the area?'

Dennis had now worked himself into quite a state, 'how the fuck should I know? I think he could know that guy who came with Peter's daughter. I did see them talking together very much as if they had met before.'

'Thank you, Mr Dennis, you have been very helpful.'

In truth, Dennis had no idea that he had just given the Inspector confirmation of a suspicion that had been nagging at him but until now without any connection.

'Bye, for now,' he said to Dennis. 'Don't go away as I may need to come back to you.'

'Are you going?' Ophelia had been looking forward to the new experience of being interviewed for murder and had done up her lipstick whilst waiting. 'Don't you need to speak with me?'

The Inspector was well up to this sort of trick and he smiled on her saying, mendaciously, 'all in good time, Madam unless you could give me the names of any friends John may have in this area.'

Of course, Ophelia had absolutely no idea as to any friends or acquaintances that her newest young man might have; so far as she was concerned it was just her, herself, who occupied John's thoughts and especially, his desires.

'Someone seems to have really had it in for him to judge by the photo taken after his death. You know the one that made your Boss chuck his breakfast up.'

'Oh dear,' Ophelia made a sort of *moue*. 'The poor boy.'

'You could say that again, Madam.'

The policeman shook his head, he was constantly astonished at the vanity of a few women, even in the midst of a murder situation.

Chapter Eleven

Back in the study, Inspector Carstairs sat down behind Peter's huge "partners'" desk, lent back in the swivel chair, spun round a couple of times (he always did this when sitting in this type of chair, as it reminded him of those peculiar spinning dodgem cars at fun fairs) before once again, wrestling with the current problem. So, where were they? He'd put out a pick-up call for Luke and was pretty sure they would get him before long.

He was soon directing one of his detectives who was on the case, 'he's medium height, well dressed, last seen wearing a cashmere sweater—dark blue, over a checked shirt, no tie, dark red fine cord trousers. Shoes? Now what was he wearing? Recollection came: 'dark brown loafers.

'Right you are Sir.'

The Inspector got to his feet, I think I'd better have a look at the room he was sleeping in. Your room I think Miss Jemima?'

Jemima had switched from being tearful and very upset at Luke's behaviour, to being very angry at being taken for a ride. 'Yes, come with me, I'll show you.

They hurried up the front stairs and then up a further rather steeper flight to Jemima's bedroom, which was in a certain amount of disorder.

'Sorry about this but I just didn't have time to sort it when I got the shout about my car.'

'That's OK Miss, I've seen a lot worse!'

Heaping a duvet lying on the floor, back on the bed, revealed a leather bag of sort of an overnight size, that lay on the floor. Before Jem could pick it up, the Inspector caught hold of her. 'No, just leave it for now.' He pulled out his phone and buzzed for one of his detectives. 'Bring your fingerprinting stuff and get yourself up to the top floor.'

'Any other of his possessions? In the bathroom, perhaps?'

The bathroom yielded little except an electric razor that the policemen doubted would tell them much but was yet another clue. However just as they were leaving the bedroom, the Inspector looked around and saw something on a small bedside table beside one side of the broad double bed. A notepad had been laid face down on the table. He picked it up, turned it over, it appeared to be blank. He got his glass (without which he had never gone anywhere since he joined the force) and there, just detectable if you were searching for something, were impressed the numbers for the safe. 'Hmm, careless' thought the Policeman, 'very careless!' He gave it to his junior who held out a plastic evidence bag. 'No word of the car?'

'Not yet Sir.'

Jemima was now furious but mostly with herself, 'how could I get so taken in?' she raged, 'I feel such a bloody fool.'

'Don't beat yourself up, Miss. It happens to lots of people.' The detective doing the prints was a nice young copper with a broad smile.

She looked briefly out of her bedroom window. 'Goodness, are you searching the grounds?' she asked young Jennings.

'Yes, Miss. It's going to take a bit of doing I thinks, but we has to be thorough.'

Chapter Twelve

Peter had gone outside to see what the searchers were up to. 'Any recently disturbed ground, probably in a sheltered position. Just in case the guy buried all or some of the jewellery.'

Jemima caught up with him, 'Dad, you'll never guess …' She told him of the Inspector's unearthing of the impressed digits. He was suitably amazed, 'seems like we've got a good guy in charge of things, doesn't it?'

A sudden shout had all the searchers looking at one of their party.

'Let's have a look, no touching, Cribbins for heavens sake!' Cribbins shrank back suitably chastened. 'Sorry Sir.'

'Photographs please. Fingerprints.' All this having been done to the Inspector's satisfaction, he put on a glove and picked up an object from the ground. It was a ring, just a small circle of large diamonds, set in white gold. 'How in Hades did you spot it?' he asked Cribbins.

'Don't really know, Sir, I think it must have just caught the light and a sort of sparkle was what I saw.'

The Inspector was looking carefully around the area; no sign of anything else. 'Do we know what he put the jewellery in—must have had some sort of bag in order to carry it all. I can only imagine that this might have fallen out of the bottom of a bag. Anyway, it all goes to show that we are on track. Let's keep it up.' It was if he had set a pack of bloodhounds on the trail as the search was resumed with redoubled vigour. It was fairly easy to follow the escapee because the grass was flattened but every now and again the trail dried up as the feet must have taken to a path.

At the end of another hour, "treasure" was found for the second time when another ring was found in the same fashion as the first; really by sharp eyes and a bit of luck. The Inspector was getting constant updates on his phone and about noon, a sighting was reported of the car, apparently heading for Dover. 'He's probably gone to Dover because although its further from here, Newhaven is so small and quiet, he'd be spotted in a trice.

'True although I doubt he'll make it through Dover unless the passport folk are asleep. Everyone has been alerted!'

Midday came and it was unexpectedly hot; 'we'll stop for a bite and something to drink.'

They all retreated back to the yard outside the kitchen where a police van was now parked.

'Oh great, the meat wagon. I hope they've got some decent grub. I could sink a couple of pints easy!' Cribbins had been hoping to be the one to find more jewellery but, so far nothing else had been found.

'Dream on, Cribbins', the Sergeant, who had been left in charge of the search party, could have done with a pint as well. 'Half an hour and then we'll start again.'

Chapter Thirteen

Jemima was sitting in a corner of the smallish sitting room that the family used when the drawing room seemed too large. She was still extremely upset. She looked down at her phone which was on the table as if it might have something to say. She had tried Luke's number several times without success. Her original upset at her boyfriend's disappearance and the discovery that he had probably just 'played her' to get access to the jewellery had fermented into rage and the earnest hope that the police would pick him up. In a funny way, she was less worried about her car, since common sense told her that, if the chips were down, the insurance company would pay up and, in the meantime, she was sure that her Dad would have some wheels that he could let her use. All the same the very thought that Luke, whom she had fallen for in a big way, was swanning about in it made her mad.

Seeing the Inspector passing the window, she rushed across the room and hailed him. 'This is Luke's phone. I expect he's frothing at the mouth at himself for having left it behind. I can't get an answer from him.'

She handed the phone to the Detective. 'Why didn't you give me this before?' he demanded. 'Oh well, we'll see what we can get from it.' His own phone burbled. 'Yes, Inspector Carstairs here.'

'What? You think you may have missed him?' he listened. 'For Christ's sake, I especially told you to look out for him. He's got one of the biggest jewellery hauls I've ever come across with him plus he's in a stolen car and you've let him go?' He listened again, 'You're sure no car of that description has come through?'

'Ostend? I suppose it's possible. You've notified the French? Let me know the instant you hear anything. I'm sending you another photo of him and, of course, it's not beyond the bounds of possibilities that he's switched cars.' A long pause, then 'Well we can't control the weather. Is it really bad? Are sailings still leaving Dover? You don't know? Well, man, for God's sake find out PDQ.' He switched off.

'Thick fog in the Channel! He's checking on sailings to Ostend. It's a slightly longer crossing.'

Jemima almost forgot her woes, as she listened in to the Inspector's phone calls. Goodness, she thought, a chase in the English Channel in thick fog; surely that didn't happen every day!

She looked out of the window. Yes, there was even a bit of fog here. Then, she heard the Inspector saying, 'OK, I'll head to Dover 'I'll bring someone who can identify him in case he's in another vehicle.'

'Get your coat,' he said to Jemima 'and hurry up.' She heard Carstairs giving instructions to his juniors as she grabbed a coat in the hall and hurried back.

Chapter Fourteen

As Jemima clambered into the back of a patrol car, she felt both an adrenalin rush and a *frisson* of fear; she'd never been in anything like a police chase before.

As if he sensed her feelings, Carstairs turned around and smiled at her, 'don't you worry Miss Jemima, we'll get the brute, no worries!'

They turned south and hit the M2, which as usual was pretty busy with endless lines of trucks heading for the Continent. Fortunately, whenever they got stuck behind an especially long train of vehicles, they could put on their blue lights.

Jemima shivered. The fog grew thicker and the traffic slowed down to a crawl. Under blue lights, they wove their way through and finally passed the very welcome sign of 'Port of Dover.'

Jem wondered to herself what they would do now; all sorts of scenarios played out in her head the most outlandish, as she eventually told herself, was that they would ram their target! Surely that only happened in cops and robbers films?

'OK, Miss Jemima?' asked the Inspector? ''Fraid the fog may hamper us. We'll have to see what our pilot has to say.'

'I'm in your hands, Inspector, but we aren't chasing him out to sea are we?'

'Depends on what we can find out from the officials here. Now, if we can only weave our way down to the harbour police who are expecting us, we will find a bit more as to what's what, I hope. This fog is no picnic, is it?' It was the thickest fog Jemima had ever seen and when she then heard the haunted wailing sound of the foghorns, she felt a shiver up her spine.

'Spooky!' she said.

They arrived at the dock where the police launches were tied alongside. A police man waved at the Inspector and he took Jemima over and introduced her. 'Come on Miss, I'll show you the boat we are using. He helped her get aboard one of the launches and suggested she go down into the small cabin to keep warm.

Carstairs went off to confer with his colleagues in the Maritime Police HQ saying to Jem,' I'll be back in a jiffy. Try not to worry. We'll get him, I promise'.

Jemima felt herself trembling and wishing fervently that she had never met Luke. He had seemed so nice, so interesting and more sophisticated than many of her present coterie of friends. She even looked back to last night before everything had gone so horribly wrong. He'd made love so wonderfully; again, she felt tears running down her cheeks. Why, oh why did he have to be a thief? She sniffed as a surge of rage threatened to overcome any warm ideas she had had about him: he'd taken her for a fool; she had been one! She wished she had got Tiff or her Dad to come with her.

Abruptly, her thoughts were brought to an end with the Inspector opening the door from the tiny cockpit.

'What's the news, have you got him, Inspector?' the words tumbled out of her.

'Not yet but, I've been told, the ferry to Ostende is lying just outside the harbour here; it's waiting to do the crossing when the fog lifts a little but we can reach it OK in the police launch.'

A terrified Jemima, 'Are you sure it's safe in the fog?'

'Don't worry Miss, they won't move unless they judge it to be safe.'

Jemima never subsequently knew how she had got through the next hour. There was a lot of shouting and the stamping of feet running on the deck and the quayside. She found two blankets which she wrapped around herself as she was now freezing cold; it was all a nightmare, unreal with the thick fog all around them and the sound of wailing foghorns.

The engine was started, she felt the thrum, thrum and was then aware of the boat pulling away from the dock.

The door to the skipper's perch in the wheelhouse, opened and Carstairs came through. 'Are you OK?'

'Sorry I'm such a wimp', she whispered, 'but I feel a total fool to be taken in by him.'

'Don't think like that, Miss. He's an animal who feeds off nice people like you. Let's hope we get him and then he will get what he deserves. If you'd like it better than being stuck down there in the cabin by yourself, you can come up here with me and the skipper.' He held a hand down.

'Oh, thank you. Goodness the fog is a bit scary isn't it?'

'Not good, I agree but we aren't going far.'

Jem was about to pull out of the venture but a little bit of steel crept in and she remembered once or twice in her life, forcing herself to do something or other and being proud of herself subsequently so, biting her lip, she now told herself firmly that she would be pleased with herself afterwards, (she hoped) she held her hand out to the Inspector who pulled her up and into a perch beside him.

Outside of the cabin, the whiteness of the swirling fog blanketed all other sound until a wailing foghorn sound; it seemed very close to them.' How do you know when someone is very near to you?'

'Radar.' He answered briefly.

'How close d'you think that one was?' Jem couldn't hide a slight tremor in her voice?'

Carstairs put his arm round her and told her she was quite safe. It was very comforting to be held like this and the girl relaxed a little.

There was a bump, a pretty big bump. 'That's the ferry. Stay exactly where you are and I will be back for you. Don't move!'

There was now a lot of shouting, swearing together with the thunder of boots on the deck, which Jem reckoned must be the ferry. She just cowered down as she had been told.

Suddenly, someone jumped onto the police boat apparently carrying a sort of duffle bag. She shrank back trying to make herself invisible as she realised it was neither the Inspector nor the pilot.

Fortunately, the guy was too busy trying to find the ignition to have noticed her sitting huddled up in the shadows. She could just see the key.

She now realised it that the man was Luke, which scared her all the more; what horror of vengeance would he wreak on her if he found her and knew she'd ratted on him.

A loud shout, 'he's on the launch'.

Swearing from Luke, who turned away from the wheel. Summoning every ounce of courage, Jemima stretched out her arm and snatched the key. Where to hide it, her brain racing, she felt the Inspector's overcoat on the seat beside her; a pocket, she fumbled and finding what felt like a hole, she stuffed the ignition key inside.

She turned back in her seat and at that moment, Luke saw her. 'What the fuck have you done with the key? Where is it for God's sake, woman?'

'What are you looking for?' Jem suddenly felt rage at this man boiling up inside her but she realised he had, thankfully, not recognised her in the almost pitch dark. Through fumbling around her and under the seat, she found something long and hard. God knows what this is, she thought, but it might do.

She gulped as he reached for her and swung the object at his head. He staggered, 'you bitch' he yelled as he fell. He not only fell, but in doing so he also hit his head on the wheel.

'Arrrh!' he crashed down, yanking Jemima down with him.

God, what have I done? Jess screamed for help and very swiftly, the pilot came in. 'What's up? We can't see a bloody thing out there in this damn fog. Never known it so thick.'

'Here, 'Jess took his hand and shoved it towards the body.

'Wowee!! You're a star!' He pushed something on his phone and a long blast sounded. The Inspector rushed in—if you can rush down the steep steps on a boat—what is it?'

'We've got him. At least your girlfriend has knocked him out, the fabulous girl!

'Is she OK. Jemima are you alright? What did you do?'

Jemima was feeling much better, much safer although her right arm was very painful. 'He couldn't find the key to start the boat because I'd taken it. Don't know why but something just told me to hide it. The trouble is that when he fell, he grabbed my arm and I think it might be broken.' By this time the little cabin's lights had been turned on, Luke had regained his wits and was in handcuffs.

Carstairs was now very much the senior policeman 'Right, what have you done with the jewellery? Come on now. It won't do you any good to pretend you didn't steal it.'

'He had a bag when he came on board. It must be here somewhere.'

'Bitch.' Luke even spat on the deck which shocked poor Jemima almost more than anything else!

Carstairs looked around and, sure enough, sitting in the corner was a duffle bag. He picked it up, having now put on gloves which he had whipped out of a pocket. 'We'll do the prints later.' He unzipped the bag and put in his hand; he pulled out a necklace which he dangled from his fingers as he looked at Luke, saying 'you're a greedy sod aren't you!' He put his hand back in and pulled out a diamond bracelet.

He fumbled around in the bag but there was nothing else in it.

Jemima prodded him. 'What about the rings? Where are the other things?'

'Ah ha, yes, of course.' He did up the zip on the bag and turned it over. Yes, there was a fairly large hole in the base and this was clearly where the rings had escaped! To repeated requests to be told what he had done with the rest of the pieces, Luke just denied all knowledge of anything else.

Occasionally, one was grateful for a hole! Jemima thought.

'OK, now we'll head back to base and get rid of this scumbag. He looked at Luke and asked, 'why did you murder John Long? Was it just that he knew too much about you? Did you plan this whole thing together, except for becoming caught out with the jewellery. Pity, that haul might have set you up for life; is that what you planned? Or is once a successful thief, always a thief?'

Even in the dim light of the cabin, Luke had gone very pale thought Jemima. Perhaps he's wondering how long a sentence he'll get; the longer the better, can't be too long, she conjectured, perhaps thirty years? No answer.

She heard a loud conversation between Carstairs and a man on the ferry, and realised they were about to head back to Dover. The fog was still thick, it was like diving into white soup as they cast off from the ferry, which had towered over them. She suddenly remembered her car.

'Where's my car? Is it on the ferry still?'

'Don't worry, we'll try and get it back to you in a few days' time. Right now, it's part of our evidence.'

'Not really sure if I ever want to see it again!'

The Inspector laughed, 'well, you can always sell it! It's a very nice little car.'

'I know, I know it's just the thought of him driving it. I know that's stupid but,' she laughed, 'you know by now that I'm just a stupid woman!'

Now the Inspector laughed too, 'it will be returned to you as good as new, I promise. I'll bring it back myself.'

Jem heard herself saying, 'Oh would you? That would be fabulous.' As she said this, she thought suddenly that she was being very pushy but she had taken a shine to "her policeman" and the thought of seeing him again was unexpectedly appealing.

'Come on let's go. Oh, where is the key? Our pilot needs it.'

'In your coat pocket! '

'I wonder how it got there, you clever woman!' He fumbled in several pockets before he found the one into which Jemima had managed to stuff the key.

Chapter Fifteen

Jem had no idea how the pilot managed to get them safely through the fog and back to the HQ of the Maritime Police but, somehow, he did, and she suddenly realised that they had reached the jetty where there were several other police boats tied up. Two more policemen arrived and took Luke off; Jem could not bring herself to look at him.

Carstairs said to her in a low voice, 'I think the next time you see him will be in Court!'

'Oh God, will I have to go to Court?' Jemima's voice trembled.

'Probably but don't you go worrying about it now, it won't be for several weeks and I shall be there to look after you. Now, I will find someone to take you home.'

'Couldn't you…?' her voice trailed away as she realised she was expecting too much from a very kind policeman.

He looked at her smiled and said, 'I expect I can tear myself away from here and, in fact, there may be one or two loose ends which I can sort out.' He shouted for one of his detectives. 'Jennings, I'm taking Miss Jemima home and I'll make sure we've covered everything we need to at Laurel Park. Get on with the paperwork concerning Mr. Hervey. It would be good to get him into Court tomorrow or the next day. OK? By the by, where is the jewellery we took off him?'

'Under my desk, Sir. What should we do with it?'

'It needs to be photographed and finger printed but we've got to find the rest of the stuff, there's much more somewhere. Try laying the pieces on a black background. Find a really posh jeweller and ask him to come here to look at the stuff tomorrow, to give us at least a rough idea as to what it's worth, if he can. Put it in the Chief's safe for the night.'

'Right you are, Sir.'

Carstairs had a warm feeling when he collected Jemima; he liked her, although he admitted to himself that he scarcely knew her, she was pretty and he felt unexpectedly protective towards her. *Slow down you idiot he told himself*!

'Sorry about using a police car to take you home but I'll probably have to bring back some of the boys and the kit they've been using. I have to tell you that that the fingerprints they got in Lady Moira's apartment together with the jewellery, even though we haven't got it all as yet, tie Hervey in conclusively with marks on the murdered man. We're doing some checks with the USA; did you know the victim was also an American citizen? His passport was in his hip pocket together with a British one and a whole bunch of British and US credit cards plus quite a wad of cash. I think he was well set up to do a quick bunk if necessary. Anyhow, we're checking out both these men; I don't get the feeling that you should shed tears over either of them. By the way, have you visited Hervey's flat in London?'

'No! But I'm pretty certain it's in Notting Hill. Of course, I never met the actor man; Dad told me Dennis had a new male actor whom he was giving a try out. I think that the great Ophelia may have had something to do with that!'

'She's quite a woman,' isn't she?'

'Yes, I think she's a bit terrifying, oversexed and over age!' Jem paused before adding, 'sorry that sounds really bitchy, doesn't it but she certainly eats younger men. In almost every production I've seen, you can tell, when there is a younger male lead, she is always quite evidently smitten.'

Carstairs, 'please use my Christian name "Rufus", at least, when I've not got my Inspector's hat on.'

Jemima felt herself blushing, 'er, OK'. She clambered into the police car saying, 'Well, no blue lights today!'

'No, not until we come across a boy racer on a motorbike!'

'Heaven forbid! I think I've had enough dramas for one day.' Silence fell as they wove their way out of Dover and onto the M2.'

The policeman, 'I think I can give you back your phone as we've got all the info from it that we can; we're holding onto Hervey's phone; it was very useful in working out Mr Hervey's life. One thing we found that was especially useful; the two men knew each so it may have been a question of two thieves falling out.'

'Gracious, do you really think so? '

'Yes, it certainly looks like that. It's quite common, you know!'

Jemima said rather tartly, 'Well, it's not the sort of information I'm likely to have, is it?'

'No, sorry, didn't think. Now, we should be at Laurel Place in forty minutes according to the sat nav. Will you be staying there for a few days?'

Yes, I should think so. You know, Dad's pretty amazing but he does need a bit of support sometimes and I've no idea what Tiff's commitments are.'

'Your Dad is a really nice bloke and I am so sorry that this should all have happened. Murder is seldom edifying and the death of that poor old lady was a bit of a shocker, too.'

'I know, she could be a bloody nightmare but you wouldn't wish her to die like that.'

'D'you think she knew she was having a heart attack and then fell and bashed her head really badly. That could have been the real cause of death, you know. If people have heart attacks, they can survive if they get help quickly but, in her case, I think it was the two things together that finished her off. It will all be clearer once we get the full postmortem report. Her wretched husband looked really wiped out with shock.'

'Ron? She bullied him mercilessly, poor fellow. Frankly, once he's got over the initial shock, I think he'll be absolutely fine and, you never know, he may find true love amongst the other residents! Stranger things have happened.'

They turned in at the main gate to Laurel Place with Carstairs saying, 'D'you know what a lucky girl you are to live in this gorgeous place?'

'I do, I do! We moved here when I was only four. Dad inherited it from his Uncle, my Great Uncle Max or to give him his whole name, Maximilian; great name isn't it?'

'Makes me think of German Arch Dukes! Did he have a brother called Ferdinand?'

They both got the giggles. Eventually, Jemima managed to say, 'you know I think you are right!'

They parked in the yard outside the kitchens and had scarcely stopped when Jennings came out of the house. 'Sir, Sir!

'Yes, Jennings what is it, for heaven's sake?'

'Well, 'puffed Jennings,' the geezers at Dover have heard from Ostende that they think they've got Miss Jemima's car.

'Excellent! Is it being sent back on the ferry? We really can't go tonight. Tell them I'll be there around 9 tomorrow morning.'

Chapter Sixteen

Peter and Tiffany had been wondering when Jemima would be back. Peter had also been quite busy helping the police still in the house to find their way to various apartments as they worked through their interviews with the residents.

Tiffany heard the swish of gravel when the police car brought Jemima and Inspector Carstairs back from Dover. She rushed downstairs and threw open the kitchen door, 'Oh Jem where have you been? I've been so worried and your phone wasn't working.'

'So sorry Tiff. Rather a lot has been going on but nothing I can't tell you about. I'm just afraid I've been very naïve or bloody stupid; not sure which, perhaps both!'

'Let's get through this bunch of coppers and then we can go into a corner and have a catch-up.'

Jemima turned to Carstairs saying, 'Tiff, you've no idea how lovely this kind policeman has been. They've got Luke—took him off the Ostende Ferry in a thick fog. Thank you again.' She smiled at the Inspector 'Shall I see you tomorrow?' She certainly hoped she would!

'I'm just waiting for a copy of the postmortem which has been completed.' He withdrew from the girls so that he could read the PM on his phone without anyone looking over his shoulder.

The PM was pretty much what he had expected, *'violently stabbed in the neck by a knife, probably a sort of carving knife. Body contained strong traces of heroin.'* During their efforts to find out something about "John Long," the police had been led to the FBI. Amongst other things, they had learned that John Long was just one of several names that the man had used.

An even more interesting fact, which had come to light, was the fact that John Long Frobisher (the latter apparently the body's former and, almost certainly, his "proper" name) had been at the University of Southern California together with Luke Hervey. Further enquiries at the University had found that both of them had been thrown out in their third year for using and dealing drugs.

The Inspector was delighted to have this information and what is more to have obtained it so easily; they had got the information about the University from a trawl of Luke's flat in London. It was fortunate that they had found this out so quickly because he had told poor Jemima that he'd been at Yale; snob! Of course, she didn't know anything about "John Long" because none of them had met the actor before the day of the play.

Rather fortunately, the discovery about all this would make the cross-examination of Luke Hervey, now they had got him, much easier because they had all the necessary proof; his worst crime certainly being the murder of his friend, John Frobisher. What was more difficult to discover was how and why had they targeted Lady Moira's jewellery.

This was put to Luke.

The realisation that he had killed his close and only friend led Luke to crumble. In a rather desperate move to possibly reduce his sentence, he more or less incriminated himself.

'Well, you see we wanted to find something that was relatively easy to sell. When I met Jemima, I learned that her home was this huge country house with some rich tenants living in apartments. I think Jem told me that one of the tenants was especially rich and had a large collection of very good jewellery. When I knew Jem was working away from home, I came to Laurel Place, and was given a tour by one of the residents, Sir Ronald, because Peter was also away.'

'Go on' prodded the Inspector.

'Of course, we chatted as he showed me around and, eventually, I just asked if it would be possible to see inside one of the big apartments so that I could get a proper idea as to what they are really like. I think I said I had an aunt who could be interested in coming to live here.'

'I feel horrible now, but I just hoped he would take me to see his own.'

'Which, of course, he did. Easy!'

Whilst we were in his apartment, I asked about security and he showed me the safe inside one of the bedroom cupboards.

The Inspector could never get over the idiocy of most of the general public, even where items of great value are involved! Accustomed as he was to hearing "confessions", true or false, Carstairs was amazed at the words that seemed to be literally hanging a noose round this man's own neck, because that was what it really amounted to. He doubted that the accused was aware that his every word was being recorded; his confession had just poured out of his mouth.

'Right. So, when did you actually take the jewellery?'

'John took it. He'd realised that Sir Ron was out of the apartment, so he nipped in when the last rehearsal of the first act, which he didn't appear in, was going on. A seasoned jewel thief, he cracked the code easily, grabbed all the stuff out of the boxes, put the boxes back and pushed closed the door to the safe. He messaged me that he'd put the stuff in a cupboard near the bottom of the stairs. As you probably know, I didn't go to the start of the performance, Jem covered for me. For some reason I panicked and realised I had to get rid of John. I think you know the rest. He was my friend, I don't know how I did it. But I did, I killed my own friend.'

All the bravado had been squeezed out of the man and he was now almost sobbing.

The Inspector switched off the recorder he'd been using.

'OK, I think you can now take a trip to the Station and, then, to a cell. I doubt you'll see the light of day for many a long year! I've recorded this conversation so I will now get it transcribed.'

Luke had never felt any remorse after burgling in the past; bizarrely, he seems to have thought that, if people were so stupid as to leave expensive "stuff" around, then why not help yourself. However, now he appeared to have found some semblance of a conscience and realised fully what he had done to Jemima let alone, his friend John. 'Could I just have a quick word with Jemima?' he asked.

'D'you really think that girl is going to want to hear your lame excuses?' Carstairs was incensed. 'You took advantage of a lovely girl and now you think one or two smarmy words will put things right?'

'I just thought……..'his voice trailed away.

'I think you'd do better to try and concoct a credible defence before you go on trial for murder plus, plus!'

The Inspector was delighted to see a look of misery in the prisoner's eyes.

He waved to Jennings, 'Take him off, caution him etc. etc. and then see he's locked up securely at the station.'

Chapter Seventeen

Once Luke had been taken off in a Police van, Carstairs suddenly said, 'I think we'd better get hold of the jewellery before one of the maids finds it when doing some housekeeping!

Summoning another of the young detectives, they were just walking to the staircase when Peter came into the hall.

'Good timing! We think we may have found the jewellery.' They reached the stairs and sure enough, there was a cupboard almost invisible in the panelling. 'Let's just hope, he wasn't telling me a whopper.' Carstairs put out his hand to open the door which was recessed into panelling so as to be virtually invisible. He was about to push it, when a small hand slipped into his free hand and he realised that Jemima had joined the little group. He squeezed it, 'Just a moment'. The door opened and they all peered into the recess.

At first glance it seemed that there was little inside except for two carrier bags for groceries: one Marks and Spencer and one Waitrose.

The Inspector looked around the little group and laughed, they all looked so glum, deflated.

'Let's see what's in the bags, shall we?'

Letting go of Jemima, he picked up the bags and, without looking inside, carried them to the big Hall table.

'Now, everyone, let's see what we have here.' The little group stood temporarily frozen, eyes fixed on the bags. 'Gloves please.'

'Is this really Lady M's jewellery?' Peter could not believe it.

'Well, we can't be certain until we see what Mr M & S and Mr Waitrose have in their bags…bags cost £1.00 you know.'

Nobody laughed at what, Carstairs had to admit, was a pretty poor joke.

'Here we go,' he put his hand in the Waitrose bag and pulled out a long necklace; the sort that you wind twice round the neck thought Jemima. He laid it on the table with the stones winking as they caught the light.

'Wow!' Jemima. In fact, nobody else spoke!

Peter suddenly thought that they really should have Ron with them; after all, they were his pieces. 'Inspector, I think we should get Sir Ron in while we're doing this, don't you?'

'Yes, absolutely! He shouted for one of his staff and dispatched him to find the poor widower.

Ron was found in the drawing room flopped in an armchair and gazing into space. 'Yes, of course I'll come.'

Back in the Hall, Jemima sat him down by the table. 'Looks like we've found the jewellery, Sir Ron!'

'Well done!' In truth, Ron was wondering what on earth he would do with the damn stuff now that Moira had gone.

He did have one idea for a couple of the pieces; for the rest, he supposed he'd have to sell it. He didn't need the money especially now that he was no longer supporting an expensive wife; time to decide that in the coming days.

He looked at the Waitrose bag as Carstairs pulled another piece out. This was a pearl choker, five strands of almost matching pearls fastened with a diamond clasp. Inspiration suddenly struck; he would give it to Anna Louise. The two of them had spent a lot of time together and he knew that she would really treasure it. In fact, he always thought that he'd have been much happier if he'd met and married her before being entrapped by Moira.

'Sir Ronald, look at this, please.' Carstairs had picked another piece out of the bag. A large diamond brooch with a sapphire set in the middle.

'Yes, yes I think I bought it at auction for one of Moira's birthdays.'

'Wow, a lucky girl!'

It took rather more than an hour to go through all the pieces but at the end of it, Ron nodded saying,' I think it's all here.'

The glittering collection, save three pieces which he left on the table, was all swept up and returned to the carrier bags. 'We can now put it back in the boxes which are all in the safe.' The Inspector felt pleased that this had gone well. 'What did you want to do with these items?' He was indicating the three items Ron had put aside.

'Don't worry about those, I have another plan for them.' He pulled the silk handkerchief from his jacket pocket and deftly wrapped the jewellery up in it. He then stuffed the package in his inside jacket pocket.

Chapter Eighteen

By mid-afternoon, the police had finished their searches and other evidence gathering and returned to the Station. The Inspector, on the pretext that there was something else he needed to check, remained behind.

'Did you tell the actor man that he was free to go?' Peter asked Carstairs. The latter, who's mind had been rather diverted, had to confess he'd forgotten about Dennis.

'Sorry, I'll do it now.' He disappeared with Jemima showing him the way.

This had not escaped her father and he said to Tiffany, 'I rather think Jem's got a new admirer.'

Tiff was feeling protective of her sister, 'Well I hope he's better than the most recent one!' Her phone burbled, 'Yes, Ron, Yes, OK. Four o'clock.'

Peter was answering the same call. 'Yes, Ron. Lovely, four o'clock! See you then and, yes, I'll try and bring Anna Louise.'

When Jemima arrived back a few moments later, she, too, announced that she was bidden to tea in the pagoda at 4 o'clock.

'What on earth is Ron up to now? I hope he's not going to tell us that he is going to commit suicide or something wild like that!'

'Don't be silly. It's not his birthday is it?'

'No, no. Well, I guess we'll just have to go and see.'

The pagoda was, indeed, the copy of a Japanese pagoda that had been constructed and put in the park in about 1780 following the journey of an ancestor to the Far East. It made a delightful spot for a picnic or a midsummers supper.

Peter established that the kitchen was preparing 'tea' to be carried out there and decided he'd put on something more suitable for the occasion than the dark suit and black tie that he had been wearing.

An hour later wearing light grey trousers, a colourful Hawaiin shirt and topped by a Panama hat, he knocked on Anna Louise's door. 'Ready?'

Anna Louise was a handsome widow in her late seventies. She had always got on well with Peter but recently her time had been very taken up in helping Lady Moira, who's demands had usually been fairly unreasonable but Anna Louise had ignored the recommendation of numerous other residents to give up the struggle. 'I could so easily have become like her,' she would say.

Peter would tease her and tell her that that was highly unlikely but she would not be moved.

By 4 o'clock, the guests had all arrived and were deciding where to sit since each side of the pagoda offered a different beautiful view. A moment later and a troop of staff from the main kitchen arrived bearing covered dishes. Georges had excelled himself with the bite size sausage rolls, tiny smoked salmon sandwiches, miniature fairy cakes, eclairs etc. It all looked fabulous!

'Can't wait to dive in,' Jem was hungry and it all looked so tempting 'but where is our host.'

Ron arrived as she spoke, so, of course, they all had to sing the dread 'Happy Birthday to You.'

'That stupid song should be banned! Never mind, tuck in everyone.' Ron was looking quite cheerful.

Anna Louise and Peter exchanged glances; they'd both thought that the Ron, who had invited them, might be very much the grieving widower, but this Ron sounded OK.

Once everyone had settled down to demolishing the delicious 'eats', Ron stood up and looking round at the others, 'You are all dear friends and in your different ways have helped me over the years. Yes, I know Moira could be difficult, bloody difficult but that did not stop our friendships.

'As you all know by now, Moira's jewellery was stolen but, thanks to this clever gentleman' he pointed to Carstairs, 'we have got it back. Now, I've come to the conclusion that, since I don't want to wear it myself, I should sell the bulk of it. However, here he drew out the package that had been bulging in his jacket.

'I have decided to keep a few pieces and I should now like to give you all a memento: for you, Anna Louise, I've chosen this pearl choker. I hope you like it and, perhaps, when you see it in your drawer or around your neck in the mirror, you will remember old Ron!'

Anna Louise looked as if she was about to burst into tears as she took the package from Ron. 'Oh, Ronnie, it's fabulous!' She gave him a hug, a shake of the head indicated that she couldn't say any more.

He drew two much smaller packages out of the wrapping; here, Tiffany this is for you and Jem, this is for you. Hope you will enjoy wearing them!'

Tiffany burst into tears swiftly followed by Jem. The latter recovered first, 'I can't think of anything to say to express what I feel, Sir Ron.'

He patted her hand, 'That's OK, my dear, tears can convey happy feelings as well as sad ones, you know.'

Jem just took his other hand and squeezed it, 'Thank you! Thank you!'

Ron laughed saying 'neither of you has opened your package yet. Could be a bunch of stones!' The girls unwrapped their packets; both contained rings and there could be little doubt, even if you weren't a jewellery expert, that they were both very beautiful and of considerable value.

They looked at each other; they looked at Peter. 'How fantastic!' Tiff said hardly able to get the words out.

Jemima reached over and took Ron's hand. She squeezed it: 'thank you!'

'Now, Peter, I don't think you wear many earrings, necklaces or even rings, do you?' They all laughed but Ron hadn't finished.

'I plan, as you might expect, to sell the rest of the jewellery but what I want to do with a part of the proceeds is to give the money to Peter so that he can have all the Turner paintings cleaned and, where he thinks necessary, reframed. I know he has wanted to do this for a long time but, as most of you probably also know, anything in the conservation department is hugely expensive; now I hope you may feel you can do what you want to, Peter.'

All eyes were now on Peter. He shook his head as if in a daze. 'Oh Ron, what can I say. It's the most generous offer I've ever had. It would be wonderful if the Turners could be cleaned up a bit; they are such fantastic paintings. Thank you, thank you!' He stood up and clapped his hands as all the others followed him. 'Let's go and look at the Turners and imagine what they'll look like once they've been cleaned up.'

Jasmine hugged Sir Ron again saying, 'I never realised that the paintings were so grubby.'

'Well!' said her Father, 'you've only seen them after I've dimmed the lights a little! No, seriously, they will look fabulous; its just that you have only seen them, as they are now, for the whole of your life. I promise you will be amazed.'

The tea party dispersed with Peter and Anna Louise going for a stroll in the water garden closely followed by Bijou and Lucifer. 'Watch out Anna Louise, they will both want to go for a swim.'

Jemima gazed after the couple, 'You know, Tiff, I wouldn't be surprised if Dad and Anna Louise don't get together now that that bossy woman is no more! What do you think?'

'I think it would be a very good thing, I really do. They are both lonely, I'm certain and I really like her!

'Me too!'